Dear Parents and Teachers:

Rourke's Adventure Chapter Books engage readers immediately by grabbing readers' attention with exciting plots and adventurous characters.

Our Adventure Chapter Books offer longer, more complex sentences and chapters. With minimal illustrations, readers must rely on the descriptive text to understand the setting, characters, and plot of the book. Each book contains several detailed episodes all centered on a single plot that will challenge the reader.

Each adventure book dives into a country. Readers are not only invited to tag along for the adventure but will encounter the most memorable monuments and places, culture, and history. As the characters venture throughout the country, they address topics of family, friendship, and growing up in a way that the reader can relate to.

Whether readers are reading the books independently or you are reading with them, engaging with them after they have read the book is still important. We've included several activities at the end of each book to make this both fun and educational.
Are you ready for this adventure?

Enjoy,
Rourke Educational Media

Isle of Enchantment

By Precious McKenzie
Illustrated by Becka Moore

Rourke
Educational Media
rourkeeducationalmedia.com

www.rourkeeducationalmedia.com

Edited by: Keli Sipperley
Cover and Interior layout by: Renee Brady
Cover and Interior Illustrations by: Becka Moore

Library of Congress PCN Data

Isle of Enchantment / Precious McKenzie
 (Rourke's World Adventures Chapter Books)
 ISBN (hard cover)(alk. paper) 978-1-63430-390-3
 ISBN (soft cover) 978-1-63430-490-0
 ISBN (e-Book) 978-1-63430-584-6
 Library of Congress Control Number: 2015933784

Printed in the United States of America,
North Mankato, Minnesota

Table of Contents

Pack Your Bags

My brother and I never stay home for long. Even though we're both 12 years old, I bet we've slept in our own rooms, in our own beds, maybe ten or 15 times. Okay, maybe I over exaggerate a bit. We're always bounding around the world, following our parents on their research trips. Our mom is a bird biologist. Our dad is a historian.

Most of the time it's pretty sweet. While Mom and Dad work, Tomas and I log onto our laptops and do our homeschool assignments even though we're thousands of miles from home. Sometimes we go on field trips. Sometimes we help with the research. Sometimes we help with camp.

Yeah, camp. For the research trips, we travel in groups with other professors and their families. We usually sleep in tents. Once in a while, we're lucky enough to travel in motorhomes. Those are nice.

They have full kitchens, an indoor shower, and real mattresses to sleep on instead of foam pads that go under a sleeping bag. Tomas says we look like a band of gypsies with laptops, binoculars, and specimen jars. But I don't mind. I think kids my age are lame. I'd rather hang out with adults.

Tonight, I'm doing laundry and packing my duffle bags for our next research trip. We're heading to Puerto Rico so Mom can study the elusive Antillean crested hummingbird. Mom is really excited about this trip, especially since it is the middle of winter here in Chicago. She told us to toss our swimsuits and flip flops in our bags—we're going to a tropical paradise.

Dad, of course, doesn't plan to spend much time on the beach. He wants to visit museums and soak up history. When he isn't teaching, or reading, he's in a museum archive. He loves museums so much he was even locked in one overnight because he didn't hear the closing time announcement. The museum guard thought everyone was out and locked up for the night. And there's Dad, reading about the Korean War, completely clueless. It was pretty embarrassing to read about him in the newspaper the next day.

"You don't know, Marisol, that we won't need long underwear," Tomas whined in my face as we packed our bags.

"Tomas. Stop. Listen to yourself. We are going to the tropics, not Siberia." My brother gets a little stressed whenever we pack for a place we've never been before. He likes to be prepared and plan for every little detail.

Tomas pushed his round eyeglasses up his nose. He scratched his forehead. Even though we're twins, we look nothing alike. Tomas is short and kind of round. His green eyes are alert and cautious. I'm tall and, as Aunt Bernadette says, athletic. Tomas's dark hair is puffy and curly. Mine is dark and straight. Total opposites but we always have each other's backs.

Tomas ran his fingers through his curls. "Fine. How about jeans? A pair? Two?"

"Sure. In case we go out to eat or something."

We both giggled at the idea. We never went out to eat. The research camps were usually hours from

civilization. We had to eat whatever was at camp: plain rice, peanut butter sandwiches, dried fruit and nuts.

"I'm sneaking candy bars in my bag." Tomas loved sweets and missed his American candy bars when we were in a jungle or desert somewhere.

"Don't do it. Mom will have a fit. She'll accuse you of trying to attract bears or something," I chuckled.

"I don't care. I am tired of canned beans and dried prunes." Tomas didn't usually challenge Mom and Dad's rules but this time I think he meant it. "I am a growing boy. I need those calories." Tomas stretched his arms and patted his belly.

"Fine. Pack those candy bars in your bags. Then, when a bear eats you alive, I will tell you I told you so."

"Marisol, how do you plan to tell me that you told me so if I am in a bear's belly?"

I tossed my bed pillow at Tomas's face.

"Shut it, smarty pants." Tomas ducked and the pillow slammed Dad in the face.

The Plan

· ·

Dad's face was a little red where the pillow hit him. He laughed it off good-naturedly.

"I hope that pillow bomb was not really meant for me, young lady." Dad tried to sound stern but the twinkle in his eyes gave him away.

"Did you guys finish packing? Your mom ran to the grocery store to pick up last minute toiletries and medicine."

"No, we're not even close. Tomas is way overthinking and trying to fit an outfit for every season in his bags."

"Always be prepared. That's my motto," Tomas snorted.

I rolled my eyes. He was such a Boy Scout.

"Tomas, Marisol, there's just one season in Puerto Rico: hot. Pack T-shirts, shorts, and bathing suits. You'll be fine." Dad was matter of fact. I could tell Mom had probably given him a huge to-do list to finish while she was out. Although he was excited about the trip, I knew there were a gazillion things for him and Mom to finish before we boarded the airplane tomorrow morning.

Tomas nodded his head and mumbled, "Okay. Fine."

"Leave room in your carry-on bag for your laptops and notebooks for school."

Tomas and I nodded. How could we possibly forget school work?

"I've got your passports and boarding passes," Dad continued, then paused, obviously trying to remember what Mom told him to tell us. "Toothbrushes? Floss?"

"Check and check," I said. "Tomas and I have our toiletries together."

"Good. Good." Dad said. "Oh, and young man, don't forget your deodorant."

Tomas blushed. I laughed so hard I almost fell off the bed. This time, Tomas aimed a pillow bomb at me and clocked me on my back.

Dad took a deep breath. "Settle down you two.

I'm supposed to tell you the plan. Listen up."

Tomas and I straightened up. We knew we needed to find out exactly what this trip was going to be like.

"We leave tomorrow at 7 a.m. and arrive in San Juan, Puerto Rico around 4 p.m., with a one hour layover in Atlanta."

Tomas and I answered in unison.

"Got it."

"That means we'll need to be at the airport at 5 a.m. to go through security. I'll wake you up at 3:30 so you can shower and get dressed."

Tomas moaned, "I don't need to shower. I need to sleep. Wake me up at 4 a.m."

"No sir. We've got a plane to catch and no time to mess around. You can sleep through the flight." Dad was all business now. "We might have time for a quick lunch in Atlanta. We'll have dinner when we get to Puerto Rico."

"Can we take snacks?" I asked Dad.

"You can buy a few when we get to the airport in the morning. But not too many. You two don't need all that junk food."

"I'm stashing candy bars in my duffle bags," Tomas muttered under his breathe. Dad didn't seem to hear him.

We heard the apartment door open and went out to the living room. Mom bustled in with her arms full of grocery bags. Snow dusted the top of her hat, coat, and boots. "Whew, I can't wait for Puerto Rico. This time tomorrow, we'll be sitting on a warm, tropical beach. Goodbye Chicago winter."

"Hello sunshine," Dad smiled. He gave Mom a kiss on the cheek and helped her carry the bags to the kitchen table.

"I think I've got everything. Vitamins, bandages, shampoo, cold medicine." Mom dug through the bags and organized the items on the table.

"I think they have grocery stores in Puerto Rico. You know, they are a US territory," I said.

"Why yes they do. But I like to always be prepared." Mom gave me her professor look that told me not to get sassy. I certainly know where Tomas got his attitude from. He is a mini-Mom.

"Did your father go over the plan with you two?"

Dad, Tomas, and I said yes.

"Good. How about the camp set-up?"

Dad cleared his throat. "No, I haven't covered that yet."

"Well then, here's how it will work." Mom gave Dad a quick look. "I spoke with the research coordinator this morning. We'll have three or four days to act like tourists while we wait for our lab equipment to arrive."

"We can soak up some history," Dad piped in.

"Yes, and then we're off to El Yunque to find the Antillean crested hummingbird." Mom was so excited she was practically glowing.

I suspected there was an important detail that Mom and Dad were keeping from us. I blurted out, "What about the camp? Do we get to stay in a motorhome since El Yunque is a United States national park?" I hoped that we could stay in Puerto Rico in comfort. It was not called the Isle of Enchantment for nothing.

Mom stuttered a bit. "Not exactly. It is a national forest not a national park. So, we get to set up a primitive camp."

That made me a little nervous. "What do you

mean by primitive? No electricity?" We'd stayed at sites without electricity before. That was not a big deal. We burned candles for lights after dark and cooked over a campfire.

"Um, yeah. No electricity and no toilets." Mom looked away from me.

"Cool!" Tomas shouted.

"Do I just find a tree if I need to go?" This situation seemed nasty to me and I was beginning to think I should just stay home for this adventure.

"Don't be silly," Mom rolled her eyes at me. "You'll dig a hole with a shovel. Cover it when you're done. It's fairly common in the backcountry. And it's called the cat hole method." Mom had evidently used the cat hole method before.

"Awesome! I get to act like a cat for three months!" Tomas was just a little too happy about this plan.

"Awesome," I groaned.

San Juan

The flight from Chicago to San Juan, Puerto Rico, was not terrible. I read most of the day while Tomas snored beside me. Mom and Dad sat behind us and mapped out our days on the island. Glancing back at them, if I didn't know better, I would have guessed that they were on their honeymoon. They looked so happy about this trip. Who would have thought it was really about work? Work in a primitive tropical rainforest, without any kind of toilet, trying to study the behavior of the smallest bird in the Caribbean? I guess my family was slightly different than most families.

Dad rented a car at the San Juan airport to take us to our tourist hotel. We would have four days to relish hot showers, soft beds, and flushing toilets. After that, we'd join the research team from the University of California in the backcountry of

El Yunque National Forest for three months of hummingbird research.

"Ready, crew?" Dad said as he dangled the rental car keys in the air.

"Let's hit it," Tomas said. Tomas was clearly ready to see the sights of the city.

Mom and Dad piled our bags in the car's trunk. Tomas and I jumped into the backseat.

"Aren't you ready for an adventure?" Tomas asked me.

"I guess so," I shrugged.

"What's the matter? Your face has been all pinched and tense looking since we got on the plane in Chicago."

Tomas knew me so well. I could rarely hide anything from him.

"I was kind of hoping for a real bed to sleep in, you know?"

Mom hopped into the passenger's seat. "What's up, kids?'

"Marisol wants luxury, a bed," Tomas chirped to Mom.

"Mari, honey, I thought you liked coming on our research trips." Mom look worried.

"I do but, I don't know. I'm just tired. Forget it." I rubbed my eyes. I was tired and maybe grouchy too. Mom rubbed my hand.

"Mari, you could have stayed with Aunt Bernadette in Chicago. You didn't have to come along if you didn't want to."

Mom's mention of Aunt Bernadette changed my mind. It would torture me to stay with Aunt Bernadette for three months. She'd wake me up at

5 a.m., drag me to yoga class three times a day, and make me eat bean sprouts and brussel sprout juice for dinner. Aunt Bernadette was a fitness freak. "No thanks."

"That's my girl," Mom smiled and looked reassured. I wasn't ready to abandon my family for a soft, warm bed.

Dad revved the engine and headed into the heart of San Juan, Puerto Rico.

The blue sky, the sparkling ocean, and palm trees were dazzling. It was so different compared to blizzardy Chicago. Cars zipped around us. Mom tried to read the road map and the road signs.

"I didn't know Puerto Rico had a big city," Tomas said.

Mom turned to him.

"Yep, high rise buildings and traffic. Just like home."

Tomas shook his head. "No, San Juan is different. It looks Spanish."

"Of course it looks Spanish," I said, narrowing my eyes at Tomas. "Who do you think settled the island in the first place?" I couldn't believe my twin could be so dense.

"I know that," Tomas said. "What I meant was that the buildings are interesting. Look at the pastel colors, the arches. It looks old and new at the same time."

"It is amazing," Dad said. I think he was trying to keep me and Tomas from getting into an argument in the car.

I shook my head and turned to look out the passenger's side window. San Juan was spectacular. It bustled with people, shops, and cafes—a fun, modern city in the middle of the Caribbean Sea.

"Why don't we find the hotel and head to the beach for sunset?" Mom suggested. Tomas fist-pumped the air.

"Yes! Let's hit the beach!"

Dad pulled the car into the hotel's parking lot. Tomas jumped out with his bags, ready to find the beach. "Slow down there, señor," Dad tugged Tomas's arm. "We're checking in and picking up the hotel room keys."

"Let's hurry. I want to swim," Tomas said impatiently.

After we checked in and went up to our room, Tomas and I didn't waste any time. We were changed into our bathing suits and ready for the beach in less than five minutes.

The beach was easy to find. It was right across the street from our hotel. The water was a calm blue like I'd never seen before. Seagulls dipped into the water, looking for food. Families ran up and down the beach, enjoying the warm sunshine.

"Tag! You're it!" Tomas pounded me on my back.

"Ouch," I screamed. Tomas raced down the shore. He knew I wouldn't let him get away with that. I sprinted after him, caught up to him, and pushed him into the sand. Instead of being angry with me, Tomas wiped the beach sand out of his mouth and eyes. He laughed and rolled away into the sea. His black head bobbed up and down with the waves. "Come in, the water's fine," he yelled. Tomas looked like a merman in the water. I dove in after him. We raced through the water like dolphins.

"I love Puerto Rico," Tomas shouted. The tropical climate certainly suited Tomas.

"Me too," I yelled back.

Mom waved at us from the shore.

"Time to come in. The sun's setting," she said. Tomas looked sad.

"Tomorrow, little brother." I rubbed my fist on top of his wet head.

After breakfast the next day, Dad suggested we try kitesurfing.

"I've got lessons all set up for us," he said.

I couldn't believe Dad would kitesurf. He isn't very athletic. Tomas and I were very excited. We walked down to the beach to meet our instructor.

"Hola, Perez family! Are you ready to fly over the water?" Fernando, our instructor, was tall and muscular.

He gave us life vests, a board that looked like a snowboard, and a harness that attached the large kite to our life vests. Tomas glanced nervously at me.

Fernando had us practice hooking and unhooking the kite from the harness. That was one way we could bail out if the ride got too rough.

"Let tu padre go first," Fernando patted Dad on the back. He led Dad to the water. We couldn't hear what Fernando said to Dad. But, the next thing we knew, Dad's kite caught the wind and off he went. Dad bounced across the waves like a rubber ball. He spun in a pattern like a tornado.

"OOO, eeee, OUCH! Aiy-yay-yay!" Dad screamed across the shoreline.

Fernando dashed across the beach, waving his arms and shouting in Spanish. In a flash, his kite unhooked from his harness and Dad's body slammed into the sea water. Fernando rushed into the water to make sure Dad was okay.

"Señor Perez, that was amazing!" Fernando must be an optimist. Dad was red-faced and looked miserable, like he had just gotten into a fist fight.

"I think I broke a rib," he said, rubbing his side.

"Want to do it again?" Fernando obviously didn't get Dad's message.

"No way, I'm too old for kiteboarding. It hurts to pound into the water."

"Niños?" Fernando looked at me and Tomas. "Want a turn?"

After watching Dad bounce like a fish out of water, Tomas and I had a change of heart. Kiteboarding didn't look like the sport for us.

Since I am older than Tomas by six minutes, I took charge. "No thank you."

"Windsurfing?" Fernando pointed to the windsurfing boards down the beach.

"Does it hurt like kiteboarding?" Tomas asked.

"No, no, it is much safer," Fernando said. He looked like he meant it.

Tomas shrugged. "Why not? It's got to be better than slamming against the waves attached to a large kite."

Fernando gave me and Tomas a lesson on windsurfing. Dad sat under an umbrella. He said he needed a rest.

Tomas and I spent the day gliding over the shallow blue water, twisting and turning to catch the tropical breezes. If the breeze slowed down, we fell over and landed in the warm water.

"Marisol, this is awesome!"

"I know! I feel like a bird," I said.

"I feel like a pirate, sailing away on my own private raft to my own private island," Tomas laughed. He has quite the imagination.

"Tomas, you're a goofball!" Just as I said it, a wave rolled in and knocked me off my board.

Dad waved to us from his beach chair. "Hey, kids, time to go get cleaned up for dinner!"

Tomas and I were starving. We'd been swimming and windsurfing all day. We devoured heaping plates of beans, arroz con pollo, which is chicken with rice, and arroz con dulce, candied coconut rice. After dinner, Mom and Dad decided that we should "soak up the local culture."

Mom found a cafe in Old San Juan that had salsa dancing. Tomas and I didn't want to dance.

"Oh, kids, it will be fun," Mom pleaded with us.

"I don't know how to salsa dance," Tomas shook his head.

"You didn't know how to windsurf and you learned," Dad chimed in.

"I don't want to dance with girls," Tomas said.

"Dance with me then," Mom suggested.

"Oh, no!" Tomas said as he backed away from Mom.

Dad said we should give Tomas a break because he is going through an "awkward phase."

"Marisol, want to dance?" Dad held out his hand to me. I shrugged my shoulders.

"Sure, why not?"

Dad and I made our way onto the crowded dance floor. People of all ages were moving to the bright, happy beat of the trombones, trumpets, and drums. I watched how the other dancers moved and tried to step like they did.

"Hey, that was my foot," Dad exclaimed when my foot landed on his.

"Sorry, I'm new to this salsa thing," I laughed.

Tomas was standing in the corner but I could see he was moving his body to the beat. Tomas can be a little shy and afraid to try things that might involve contact with a girl. Dad and I kept dancing and he laughed to me, "I can't believe you'll still dance with your old dad. I was afraid you were too cool for that."

Dad spun me around and that's when I saw her. A small dark-haired girl was standing next to Tomas, whispering in his ear. Tomas was blushing. She took his hand and led him to the dance floor.

"Would you look at your brother? He's dancing

with a girl," Dad grinned.

Tomas stumbled around the dance floor at first. He couldn't even find the beat of the music. The girl held his hands and showed him how to move his feet and hips. He bumped into the other dancers and muttered a few "Oh, I'm so sorry." Tomas looked nervous and very sweaty. But the girl smiled as she taught Tomas how to salsa.

"May I have this dance," Mom asked as she stepped between me and Dad.

"Yes, please," I answered as I handed Dad off to Mom. I wanted to watch Tomas dance with a mystery girl and that was hard to do while I was dancing with Dad. I moved off to the corner so Tomas would not catch me watching him.

After three or four songs, Tomas started to get better. He stayed with the beat most of the time and he wasn't bumping into every other dancer on the floor. He began to look like he was having some fun.

Then his mystery girl leaned into him, placed her hands on his cheeks, and planted a kiss on his face. Tomas lost the beat and skidded into his dancing partner. He looked surprised. The girl ran off.

Tomas rushed off the dance floor in the opposite direction. I dashed after him.

"Tomas, hey, wait up," I called.

Tomas was outside in the fresh air by the time I caught up to him.

"What happened in there, little bro?" I asked.

"I don't know. One minute I'm learning how to dance, the next I get kissed." Tomas was embarrassed.

I laughed, "You act like you've never been kissed."

"I haven't," Tomas confessed.

"Seriously?" I asked.

"Seriously," he answered.

Wow. Tomas's first real kiss was with a total stranger. Tomas shrugged sheepishly. "Maybe I am cuter in Puerto Rico than I am in the United States?"

I shook my head.

"Nope. Don't think so." Who am I to lie to the boy?

"It must be your stunning dance moves," I told Tomas. He looked like he believed me.

A shadow moved behind Tomas. I motioned to him to be quiet. The shadowy figure came closer. Under the lamplight, I recognized the girl from the dance floor.

"Tomas, someone's looking for you," I sang.

Tomas turned around and jumped back, startled. The girl came closer to us.

"Hola," she said. "Tomas, you can't leave without giving me your phone number."

Even though it was dark outside, I could see the blush rising in Tomas's cheeks.

"Uh, yeah, sure," Tomas stammered.

The girl handed him her phone and he typed his contact information.

"Aren't you going to introduce me to your girlfriend?" I said.

Tomas looked embarrassed and confused.

"Carmen, this is my twin sister, Marisol." Tomas paused and motioned to me. "Marisol, this is my friend Carmen."

I stuck my hand up, waved, and offered a polite, "Nice to meet you."

Carmen did the same.

"Would you like to see real, traditional dancing?"

Carmen asked.

"Sure," Tomas agreed to anything.

"Come on," Carmen said, pulling Tomas by the hand. I trailed behind.

Carmen twisted and turned through the city streets until we came to a small restaurant.

"Here we are. Real Spanish dancing. Take a peek," Carmen said as she swung open the doors. We walked inside.

The restaurant was packed with people gazing at the stage. A guitarist strummed a few chords in the corner. A tall woman in a red ruffled dress stood in the center of the stage.

"Just in time," Carmen said. "She hasn't started the dance yet."

As the guitar played slowly, the dancer waved her arms in the air, keeping pace with the guitar.

"What is she doing?" I asked.

"She's a Flamenco dancer," Carmen said.

"A what?" Tomas asked, puzzled.

"Flamenco. It is a dance from Spain. People all over the Caribbean love Flamenco," Carmen said breathlessly.

The guitar played faster. The dancer arched her back and stomped her high heels to the beat. She spun, arched, and dipped to the rhythm of the music. Instead of slowing down, the music went faster. The dancer pounded the floor with her feet. She grasped the edge of her dress and dipped to the music.

"Isn't Flamenco beautiful?" Carmen asked us.

"Incredible," I answered.

"Come on, let's dance!" Carmen pulled me to the corner of the stage. Soon other women came to the stage to dance, too.

"I don't know how," I shouted over the music.

"Watch me." Carmen arched her back. "Now feel the music." I mimicked her moves, stomping and waving my arms to the rhythm of the song.

"Loosen up and have fun," Carmen laughed.

I was self-conscious but I tried to forget that a hundred people were watching us.

When the song ended, we left the stage.

"That's a little harder than salsa dancing," I laughed to Tomas. "It's intense."

Tomas smiled at Carmen.

"You looked great up there," he said shyly.

"Thanks," she answered. "I should. That dancer is my mom."

Tomas and I were stunned.

"I've been dancing since I could walk. Music is in my blood."

Carmen wiped the sweat off her forehead. "We'd better head back. Your parents will wonder what happened to you."

We strolled through the Puerto Rican streets. On our way, Carmen shared stories about the island. She'd been to the mainland once but missed the sunny, happy Puerto Rican beaches and the music filled nights.

"I hope you enjoy Puerto Rico," Carmen said to us when we returned to the cafe. She leaned toward Tomas and kissed him again. "You better keep in touch, Tomas. Do not forget about me." Tomas blushed. Carmen dashed off to return to the restaurant.

Arecibo Observatory

"The night life in San Juan is wild," Dad said. We only danced until midnight but many people dance until two or three in the morning on the weekends, he told us. Dancing is the nation's favorite pastime. Mom let us sleep in and catch up on our rest the next morning. We'd had a few busy days and she didn't want grouchy kids.

Mom wanted to see the Arecibo Observatory, home of the world's largest radio telescope.

Since it was a science thing, Mom was completely excited.

"Do you kids realize how awesome the radio telescope is?" Mom asked.

"Um, hum, sure," I replied.

"I don't think you do." Mom turned on her professor mode.

Mom held up her hand and pointed her finger,

"Number one, it discovered the rotating rate of the planet Mercury. Number two, it made the first radar surface maps of Venus. Number three, it discovered the first planets outside of our solar system. Number four, it discovered ice on Mercury's north and south poles. Number five —"

"Honey, we get it. The radio telescope helped scientists make big discoveries. Now can we take the guided tour?" Dad interrupted.

Mom looked irritated but she agreed to let the tour guide teach us this time.

I have to admit the tour was cool. But Mom found a group of scientists who were beginning new research with the telescope. She waved us away. That was her signal that she would be a while and that we could go ahead without her. Dad decided to have a snack. Tomas and I wanted to explore the area. The entire observatory area looked like something out of a James Bond movie, tall platforms, antennae, and wire cables in all directions.

"Tomas," I whispered. "Look over there at that cable car. I bet it goes all the way to the top."

Tomas nodded, "It's probably only for scientists."

"We're almost scientists," I reasoned. "One of our parents is a scientist. I think that counts."

Tomas was not convinced.

"Come on, let's hop in and go for a ride. Nobody will miss us and nobody will see us." I wanted to see the observatory from a bird's eye view, the very top of the dome.

Without waiting for Tomas's answer, I jumped into the rectangular cable.

"Mari, you're crazy!" Tomas hissed at me. Then he jumped into the cable car, too. We traveled slowly up the cable, inching closer to the telescope's receiver dome. The tropical parrots' songs echoed through the trees around us.

"Tomi, isn't this incredible? We can see everything!"

"Mari, stop jumping up and down! You're shaking the car!" Tomas didn't really like heights.

"Tomi, this is what birds see! Don't you wish you were a bird?"

"No. No, I don't. Now stop rocking the car! You'll break the cable. Then we'll plummet to our deaths."

"Oh, stop it you worry wart. Enjoy the view!" I

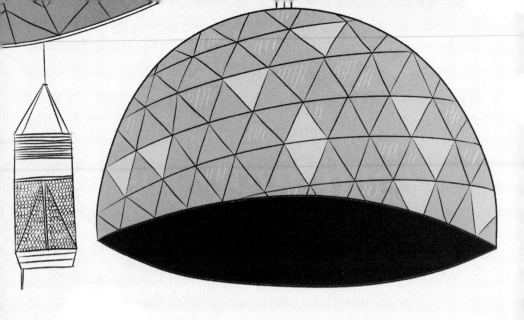

hated it when Tomi got all chicken.

A loud rusty screech stopped our argument.

"What's that?" Tomas asked.

Again we jerked around in the cable car, and heard a metal-on-metal scraping noise, followed by a sharp stop. The stop was so abrupt, it knocked me backward and almost over the edge of the cable car's railing.

"Mari! It stopped! It stopped! We're stuck," Tomas was in panic mode.

"Hush, Tomi. We're fine. It stopped for a minute. It will start again soon." I didn't know when exactly it would start. I just didn't want Tomas to start crying. He was really annoying when he cried. Big blobby boogers always got smeared all over his face. Disgusting.

"No, it won't be fine, Mari. We'll be up here for days, months, years. They'll forget about us and we'll starve to death."

Tomas looked down at the forest below us. "We're going to die!" he cried harder. Tears splashed down his round cheeks. His sobbing shook the entire cable car. He was a mess.

"Tomas, listen to yourself. Don't be stupid. Mom would send out a search party before any of that would happen." Tomas's imagination could run wild.

"Mari," he moaned. "We'll die here."

"You are acting like a big old baby. Now calm down," I commanded. "And think of a plan."

Tomas took deep breaths. He wiped his nose on the back of his hand.

"Yeah, you're right. Mom would look for us. She wouldn't just leave us."

"That's right. Mom would never leave us," I said.

Finally, he was pulling himself together. Am I the only mature person in this family?

"Why don't we climb out of the car and climb down the cable to the station?" Tomas suggested.

"Tomas, there's no way we could hold on and make that climb."

"I'll do it and send help for you," Tomas looked serious.

"You can't. You're not strong enough," I said.

"Mari, what options do we have?" Tomas was ready to get out of the cable car that was dangling in mid-air.

I reached in my back pocket. "I can call Mom," I said as I waved my cell phone in his face. Tomas looked stunned.

"You've had your phone the whole time?" he said.

"Tomas, settle down. Let me handle this."

I dialed Mom's number. It went to voicemail. She was probably still talking to the scientists. I glanced at Tomas, made a sad face, and mouthed "Voicemail."

"Leave a message," Tomas insisted.

I left my message: "Um, Mom, hi. This is Marisol. Tomas and I are uh in a little situation. We're actually stuck. Really stuck. In a cable car."

"Up high," Tomas added as he leaned into the phone, "by the dome."

Beep. End of message.

"There. I'm sure she'll call back," I said with false confidence to Tomas.

"What if she left her phone at the hotel?"

"Fine, Tomas. I'll call Dad."

I dialed Dad's cell phone. It also went to voicemail.

I left the message: "Hi Dad, everything's fine but, um, Tomas got us stuck. Can you help us get down?"

Beep.

"I got you stuck? It was your bright idea, not mine," Tomas huffed and turned away from me.

He curled into a ball and buried his head under his arms. He started to sob.

"We're going to die up here," he wailed.

"Oh shush and wait for Mom or Dad to call back," I hissed at Tomas.

The wind picked up and rocked the cable car. Tomas cried louder. I sat down next to him and put my arm around him.

"Tomi, chill. They will find us."

He looked up at me.

"When?"

"Soon."

We sat in the broken cable car for three hours. No one came to look for us except a flock of bright Puerto Rican Amazon parrots. The curious green parrots landed on the cable car's railing. They turned their heads, sang to each other, and hopped from railing to railing. One leaped onto Tomas's head. It pulled at his hair. Another leapt onto my head and chewed on my earrings.

This made Tomas laugh.

"They must think we're weird for sitting up here all day. Like we think we're birds."

"Yeah," I agreed, "I bet those parrots think we're bird-brained."

We heard shouting from down below.

"Mari! Tomi! Where are you?"

It was Mom. Tomas and I jumped up and waved

over the railing. The cable car swayed a bit. But Mom saw us. She was with people wearing uniforms and hard hats. The uniformed people did not look happy.

"Babies! Are you all right?" Mom shouted.

"Yes," we yelled back.

"Hold on! They are going to re-start the cable. Brace yourselves!"

We nodded and waved to Mom to signal that we understood. I grabbed Tomas's hand.

"Hold onto the railing and hold tight to my hand." The cable car lurched backward. Tomas and I collided into each other. "Hang on," I told him, "We'll be back on the ground in no time." And we were. Unfortunately, when we got down to the ground, the uniformed men said something to Mom in Spanish. Mom did not look pleased.

Mom turned to us, "Tomas, Marisol, come. You have some explaining to do to these gentlemen."

Tomas and I were in big trouble. The men led us into an office. For about an hour, they explained to us how much danger we faced. They also threatened to call the police. Mom convinced them that we were sorry. And that we wouldn't do anything like this, ever again.

"Now, you apologize kids," Mom nudged me in the ribs.

"Señors, we are so sorry. I, we, we didn't mean to cause trouble," I stuttered. The men, who were security guards, did not smile.

"Sirs, we were just having such a good time, we wanted to see it all up close," Tomas added.

Tomas and I were sincere. We felt lucky to be back on land safely. The security officers were silent.

One of the officers cleared his throat and looked down his nose at us, then turned to Mom.

"Señora, We will not press charges or make you pay a fine," he said.

"Thank you, gracias," Mom smiled and reached out to shake their hands.

"Señora, please make sure your children do not do something as reckless as this in the future."

"Yes, sir, sí. Gracias, gracias." Mom was practically bowing and kissing their hands.

One of the men led us outside. Then Mom turned to me and Tomas.

"I will think of a punishment for the two of you. Never do something like that again. You could have gotten hurt." Mom's eyes were fiery like a dragons. She paused, caught her breath, and continued, "For starters, you're going back to the hotel for an early bedtime."

"Mom!" Tomas started to argue with her. Tomas wanted to go dancing again, to see if he could find Carmen, the girl who kissed him the night before. When Tomas saw Mom's hand go up in the air, Tomas decided against arguing with her.

El Morro

Because of our mistake at the observatory, Mom and Dad agreed that we would have to be punished. Our laptops were taken away, except for school work time, and we now had a strict eight o'clock bedtime. We would be fine without the laptops. The eight o'clock bedtime was the worst. Tomas and I couldn't go out dancing in the evening. We missed watching all the funny night time television shows. We felt like kindergarteners again, bath and bedtime by eight o'clock sharp. Boring!

We were still allowed to go out and explore the island, but only with Mom and Dad. Dad wanted to soak up the history of Puerto Rico. He planned a day at El Morro, a fort by the sea. El Morro is an old Spanish fort that was built to protect the island from pirates and invaders. It's about four hundred years old. It sits on a cliff overlooking the water.

In El Morro, we watched a movie about the history of the fort, took a guided tour, but Dad was anxious to explore the fort more on his own, at his own pace.

"Come on, kids," Dad said, "Let's go see the canons!"

Tomas got excited.

"Can we shoot canons?"

"No. Don't even think about it," Dad laughed.

I have to admit, El Morro is pretty cool. We climbed six levels of the fort. From the top of the fort's wall, we looked out to the Atlantic Ocean.

"Wouldn't it be awesome to blow up pirate ships from here?" Tomas asked.

"Yeah, but it is kind of creepy," I said.

"Why do you say that?" Tomas looked puzzled.

"Well, think of all the people who must have died around this fort, fighting for Puerto Rico."

Tomas moved closer to me and whispered, "What are you afraid of? Ghosts?"

I kicked him in the shin and walked away.

"Ouch!" he yelled.

"Tomi, Marisol!" Dad shouted as he jogged across the fort.

Tomas and I turned to Dad.

"Kids, I'm going to speak with the park ranger. You two can keep exploring. Just stick together, all right?"

We told Dad we'd be fine. We knew he wanted to talk about history with the park rangers. He was probably working on a new article or book project and needed to find out more details from the rangers.

"Mari, let's go to the Old Tower. I hear it's haunted," Tomas said.

I knew he was playing a game with me, to see if I was afraid. I wasn't going to let him win this game.

"Okay. You lead the way," I agreed.

After crossing the fort, we found Torre Antigua, also known as the Old Tower. We walked through a crumbling tunnel. The lights inside made an eerie green glow. It felt like a dungeon.

"Ooohhh, eeeeeee," Tomas whispered as he crept behind me. I nudged him with my elbow. He stopped pretending to be a ghost. I took my cell phone out of my pocket. I pretended to use its light to help me see in the dark tower.

"Tomas, look at this," I said, pointing the light. "It's shell damage to the fort."

"Yeah, Dad said there's artillery shell damage from the Spanish-American War," Tomas said like a know-it-all.

"The damage was caused by the United States in 1898," he added.

"Yes, I knew that," I fibbed.

"The United States won Puerto Rico from Spain in that war."

"I knew that too," I snapped at Tomas.

By this time, I was annoyed with Tomas. He thinks he knows everything.

"Let's go find Dad. I'm hungry," I said.

As we turned to leave the tower, we heard the sound of metal rattling, like heavy chains clinking against each other.

"What's that?" Tomas whispered. He looked worried.

"Shh. Be still," I whispered back to Tomas.

I wanted to find out where the sound was coming from. We heard it again, louder this time.

"Come on, let's see what it is," I said as I tugged Tomas's sleeve.

"No way, it sounds like a ghost," he said.

"So? You're not afraid of ghosts." I replied.

He didn't say a word. He looked pale and nervous.

The chains rattled again. Then we heard a low moan.

I moved in the direction of the sound.

"Marisol, no! I think this fort is haunted," Tomas said as he pulled my hand back toward him.

"Tomas, come on! We might see a real ghost!"

"Mari, no, please, don't go into that tunnel!"

Tomas cried.

I didn't listen to him. I sprinted into the dark tunnel.

"Mari!" Tomas screamed, "Mari, don't leave me behind! The ghost will get me!"

Tomas bolted into the tunnel after me. What he saw next caught him off guard.

Dad and a park ranger were hiding in the dark tunnel, rattling metal chains, and I was doubled over laughing.

After Tomas realized that we had played a practical joke on him, he half-smiled and tried to act brave to hide his embarrassment.

"Yeah, I knew you were playing a trick all along," Tomas said to me. "I know there's no such thing as ghosts."

"Mmhmm, sure," I said.

"I wasn't really scared," Tomas insisted.

I laughed again, remembering the terrified look on his face when he heard the rattling chains.

"Sure," I chuckled.

Tomas started to get angry. He knew he couldn't fool us.

"Even if I was scared, which I wasn't, why would you do that to somebody?" he said.

I smiled and shrugged.

"That's what big sisters are for."

Caves

Tomas was angry with me the rest of the day for scaring him at El Morro. What puzzled him most was how I pulled off the practical joke.

"How did you get Dad and the park ranger involved?" Tomas asked me after dinner.

"I sent Dad a text message while we were in the tower. I told him I wanted to play a joke on you because you think you know everything."

Tomas look surprised.

"And Dad agreed to do it?"

"Yep. He likes to have fun too, you know."

Tomas and I were stuffing our backpacks for a day at the caves. We had one more day to be tourists until we needed to join the research team in El Yunque National Forest.

"What do you think the caves will be like?" he asked.

Tomas shook his head and rolled his eyes. Mom popped her head into the doorway.

"Kids, it's eight o'clock. Time for bed."

Tomas and I groaned. When we got to El Yunque we would be off the hook, Mom said. That meant just two more nights of this ridiculous eight o'clock bedtime routine.

We left for the Camuy River Caves at sunrise. Dad wanted to get there earlier so we would have all day to go through the caves.

All four of us were surprised at the beauty around the caves. There were green tropical ferns and wild parrots.

"Come on," Tomas said, pulling my arm. He couldn't wait to explore one of the world's largest caves.

"Slow down," Mom told him. "We have all day. There's no rush." Mom did not like it when we got impatient.

Dad spoke up.

"Let's try to stay together. There's about ten miles of trails down there," he said.

"And many caves that haven't even been explored

yet," Mom added.

As soon as we entered the caves, we weren't disappointed. We passed stalactites and stalagmites that were probably millions of years old. The main cave's chamber felt like we were standing in a giant cathedral.

"Tomi, look up," I said, nudging him. "This cave must be six or seven stories tall, like a skyscraper."

Tomas nodded.

"I had no idea that the cave would be so large inside. I always thought caves were small and cramped," he said.

We followed the concrete trail as it wrapped around the rock formations. We could hear water.

"Look, Mari, daylight," Tomas said.

Soon we were back out in the sunlight, gazing at a giant sinkhole. Plants grew up the rocky sides. Looking up, we saw blue sky. Looking down, we could see the Camuy River.

Tomas and I gasped. "Wow," we said at the same time.

I pulled out my cell phone and took pictures from every angle.

"Mari, let's go see some more."

I nodded. We lost Mom and Dad, even though we originally promised them that we would all stick together.

"Let's see if we can find Mom and Dad too," I suggested.

I led the way but I think I took a wrong turn. We came to a dark dead end. I could feel water dripping on my head and water soaking into my tennis shoes.

"Tomi, I think I took the wrong path. This isn't the way we came in."

"Look, there's a light over there. Come on," he said.

The light we saw came from an opening in the top of the cave.

"Well, Tomi, if we could jump four stories high in the air, we could get out that way," I said.

"There's got to be a way to the main chamber," he said, scratching his head.

We walked around in circles for what seemed like forever.

"Tomi, can we sit down for a minute? I need a drink and a snack." I sat on a damp rock. I unzipped my backpack and found a bag of chips.

"Sure. If you share some with me."

I had two cans of soda in my backpack. I popped the top of my can open. Then I tossed Tomas his can. Except he missed the catch in the darkness. The soda can hit the cave wall hard and ricocheted to the floor. A high pitched shriek and the sound of thousands of wings surrounded us.

"Wha—wha—what?" I stammered.

"Bats! Run, Mari, run!" Tomi grabbed my hand. "Cover your head! And run!"

"They're touching me!" I squealed. I could feel their little leathery wings brush against my hair as they flew in circles around the cave. "Get me out of here!"

Tomas and I ran in circles, searching for a way out.

"How did we get in here?" he yelled. I knew he was scared too. The bats kept flying over our heads. We couldn't find an exit. The noise we made woke them up.

I was out of breath and terrified. "Tomi, I can't run anymore. Please stop!" I grabbed my side.

It hurt. I dropped to the ground. Tomi was right beside me.

"What do we do now?" I gasped.

"I don't know," he admitted.

We sat on the floor of the cave, unsure of what to do next.

"Keep your head covered with your arms," he whispered to me. I did. The bats dipped and swooped around us. I prayed they wouldn't land directly on us.

"Be silent. Be still. They should go away," Tomas said quietly. Gradually, the bats began to slow down. Little by little, they returned to the crevices high up in the cave walls.

"Do you think they're gone?" I whispered. I could barely see Tomas's face in the darkness even though he was sitting right next to me.

"They're not gone but maybe they went back to sleep. Get up very slowly. Be quiet," he said.

"Let's feel along the wall, to see if we can find the way we came in here," Tomas suggested.

"All right," I agreed.

It took us a long time, but we found the opening.

Then we found the concrete trail system.

"You look horrible," Tomas told me.

"So do you," I said. Tomas was dirty, wet, and his hair was standing straight up.

We followed the trail out of the darkness. When we made it out into the full daylight, we found the picnic area. "Let's sit here and wait for Mom and Dad," Tomas said.

It sounded like a good idea. Until I thought about it a little longer.

"Tomi, if they find us like this, all wet and messy, they'll know we got into trouble. Then they'll ground us again."

Tomas thought for a second.

"I can't handle any more eight o'clock bedtimes. Let's get ourselves cleaned up."

"To the bathrooms!" I declared. "Use the soap and water to scrub the dirt off yourself. Then take some of the water from the faucet and smooth your hair down. I've got a brush in my backpack."

Tomas nodded and took off.

"Oh! Hey!" I shouted after him. "Hurry. We don't know when they'll come out of the cave tour."

I've known Tomas since before we were even born and I've never known him to move so quickly. He came out of the bathroom, sparkling clean, in less than five minutes. I rushed into the women's bathroom, washed up, wet my hair, and tied it up in a ponytail.

Our clothes were still wet but maybe we could blame it on the dripping water in the caves.

"Now what?" Tomas asked.

"Now we settle down and wait like nothing happened," I told him.

Mom and Dad exited the cave about a half hour later. They found us sitting calmly in the picnic area.

"Act cool. Nothing happened, remember?" I whispered to my brother. He nodded.

"Hi kids," Mom chirped. "Wasn't that awesome?"

Tomas and I looked at each other. We smiled.

"Amazing," I gushed.

"So cool," Tomas agreed.

Dad was so proud of himself for picking such a great day trip.

"I knew you kids would love it!" he said, a massive

grin spreading across his face.

As we walked back to the car, I leaned close to Tomas so Mom and Dad couldn't hear.

"I will always, always, always hate bats."

El Yunque

After breakfast the next morning, we loaded our bags into the rental car. It was time to leave the tourist life behind and join the research team in El Yunque. Mom was beyond thrilled. She couldn't wait to track the elusive Antillean crested hummingbird. I was not ready to leave hot showers and a soft bed. But there really wasn't any choice. We came to Puerto Rico for Mom's work. And her work was in the forest.

The camp was small. There were less than a dozen tents in a circle. A few pickup trucks were parked behind the tents.

"Hola!" called a woman with bright red hair as we got out of the car.

"Hola!" my mother waved back at her.

It was Dr. O'Malley, a biologist from California. Mom had worked with Dr. O'Malley a few years ago in Tanzania. They were good friends after that adventure.

"It's nice to have you on the team, Carolina," Dr. O'Malley said, giving my mom a hug. "Oh my, look at the twins! How grown up you both are!" Dr. O'Malley gave us hugs, too.

"Alberto! You don't age! It's good to see you again," Dr. O'Malley said as she hugged Dad.

She stepped back and smiled warmly at all of us.

"Come, let me show you around camp,"

Dr. O'Malley led us to the food tent, the medical tent, and the lab tent. Everything was clean and in working order.

"Here are my research assistants, Jake and Ben," Dr. O'Malley introduced us to two college students. They must be good workers, I thought, if they could set all this up in two days.

Mom smiled and shook their hands, "Nice to meet you. I'm Dr. Perez, this is my husband, Alberto, and our twins, Marisol and Tomas."

"Nice to meet you," Tomas and I said. Mom and Dad expected us to be on our best behavior.

"We're going to unpack, then I'd like to hear

about your work so far," Mom told Ben and Jake.

"Sure. Your tents are on the left," Ben said.

The tents were set on wood platforms to lift us off the wet ground. Mom and Dad took one tent. Tomas and I shared another. There was no such thing as having your own room on a scientific expedition. We tossed our duffle bags in the tents. All food had to be stored in the food tent. Food was always locked up tight in animal-proof containers.

Mom joined the research team to go over their notes and make plans.

"Well, kids, what do you feel like? A little homeschooling or a dip in the waterfall?" Dad asked.

"The waterfall!" we whooped.

Dad drove us to the La Mina Falls. Tropical palms and ferns enveloped us. Water plunged off the side of the mountain into the pool below.

Tourists splashed into the pool.

"Hop in," I yelled to Tomas as I slid into the water. It was cold but felt wonderful.

Tomas, Dad, and I chased each other around the pool.

"I think we're going to have a nice stay in El Yunque," Tomas said.

"Me too," I nodded.

Dad let us swim another hour until we needed to head back to camp. During a research trip, everyone had to pitch in and help. We needed to get back to camp to help cook dinner.

Without electricity, cooking was basic and took a lot of time. We boiled water for rice. Dad boiled more water as he dropped hot dogs into the pot. Sliced papaya and mango served as a side dish. Dinner was nothing fancy.

Mom and Dr. O'Malley planned to hike deeper into the forest tomorrow to track the Antillean crested hummingbird. Dad said we would stay in camp, study, and handle mess duty—meals and clean up.

"Sounds like a plan," Dr. O'Malley said. "Now, let's have some dessert!"

Jake threw more logs on the campfire.

"I've got marshmallows," Dr. O'Malley said. I knew why she and Mom were such good friends. They both liked roasted marshmallows.

When we'd eaten our share of the sticky treats, Mom thought it was time for bed.

"We've had a busy few days. Let's call it a night," she said quietly as she rubbed my back.

I leaned in for a hug.

"Are you having fun, baby?" Mom asked.

"Mmhmm," I nodded.

"Good. Let me show you how to dig a cat hole for a potty."

My heart sank. Goodbye public restrooms. Hello cat hole. Hello little shovel.

"Watch out for snakes and you'll be fine," she assured me.

Camping in El Yunque was not what I expected. The forest is actually a rainforest—rain being the key word. It poured nearly every day. Mom said El Yunque receives almost 250 inches of rain each year.

Tomas and I became accustomed to being damp. The raised wooden platforms kept the bottoms of our tents from getting soaked. But rain dripped through the roofs. Nights in the rainforest were not quiet. Coquí frogs sang *coo-key coo-key coo-key* all night, along with hundreds of insects.

Dad put us on a study schedule, but most days, after breakfast duties and school work, he would take us to La Mina Falls and let us swim. Dad called it our PE class. Mom, Dr. O'Malley, Jake, and Ben spent the days looking for the Antillean crested hummingbird. In the evenings, they would input their data into the computers to track the birds' habits.

Tomas and I had free time to explore the rainforest, too. Armed with binoculars and a

camera, we learned how to identify native birds and plants.

During one hike, Tomas asked me if I wanted to catch a snake.

"Not really," I told him. I used to like to catch snakes and frogs. Not anymore.

"Come on, we could catch one and keep it as a pet."

"Mom doesn't believe in making wild animals into pets," I said.

"So? She'll never know." Tomas smiled and took an empty glass jar out of his backpack.

"No way," I said. "Count me out."

"Fine," he said. "I'll be back with the biggest snake in the rainforest." Tomas huffed and stomped away.

"Fine," I said to his back.

I propped myself against a large rock and took my book out of my backpack. I liked to spend quiet time reading a good book.

I'm not sure how long I read before Tomas came back. He strutted up to me with an itsy bitsy coquí frog in the jar.

"Mari! Look! I didn't catch a snake. But isn't he cute?"

"He is for a frog," I said.

"Kiss him and he'll turn into a prince," Tomas laughed.

"No thanks. I don't want warts."

Rain started to fall through the tree canopy.

"Well, we're wet again," I said to Tomas.

"Should we hike back to camp?"

"No, we can sit here for a while. We'll be wet wherever we go," I said.

"Ouch! The rain drops hurt!" Tomas moaned.

I looked at him quizzically.

"What do you mean it hurts?" I asked. Then a drop hit my head.

"Ouch!"

"Mari! Look up!" Tomas grabbed my upper arm. "It's raining frogs!" he shrieked.

"YUCK!" I squealed. "I'm out of here!"

I jumped up to run back to camp. I didn't want coquí frogs landing on me. Tomas opened his glass jar to catch the frogs. As he did, the one in the jar hopped out and disappeared into the mud.

I grabbed Tomas's arm. "Let's go," I cried. "This is disgusting!"

When we got back to camp, Tomas told Jake and Ben all about the rainstorm of frogs.

"It was so awesome," Tomas exclaimed to Jake and Ben. "There were frogs falling from the sky!"

"It is pretty cool." Ben said. "Do you know why that happened?"

Tomas and I shook our heads. I thought it might be something out of a scary movie.

"When it's very humid the coquí try to climb higher into the trees. Tarantulas wait for them up there, to eat them. Instead of becoming a tarantula's dinner, the coquí leap out of the trees," Ben told us.

"So, we were the frogs' landing pad?" Tomas asked.

"Yep, more or less," Ben answered.

"I want to take a hot shower and wash frog slime off me," I shivered.

Mongoose!

Occasionally, Mom let me and Tomas tag along when she went into the field. Today, she needed us to help her record the egg hatching of an Antillean crested hummingbird. We set up three cameras around the perimeter of the nest. We were careful not to disturb the mother bird or the nest.

"Looks great, kids. Now we just sit and wait for those two eggs to hatch."

"Got snacks?" Tomas asked. He was always hungry.

Mom took out dried apricots and granola bars from her backpack. Tomas rolled his eyes at me. He was tired of healthy snacks. But he was stuck with it because ants devoured his candy supply two weeks ago.

"How long until the eggs hatch?" I asked Mom.

"I've been watching this nest and calculating the

hatch date. We'll wait here the rest of the afternoon. If they haven't hatched we'll leave the cameras in place and come back to check on them tomorrow."

Sitting around and waiting all day didn't sound like fun. Mom could probably tell by the bored look on my face.

"Hey, why don't you kids take a short hike? I'll watch the nest."

As Tomas and I turned to walk into the forest, I saw a small dark shadow dart into the bushes near one of the cameras.

"Mom, what was that?" I asked.

"What?" she said.

"Something just ran into the bush," I whispered.

Beady eyes and a pointy snout poked from the bush. Its nose twitched. It must have smelled our snack. It crept around our backpacks.

"Step back slowly," Mom whispered.

Tomas and I nodded our heads. We backed away from our packs. The creature stopped scavenging and glared at us.

"That's a freaky rat," Tomas whispered.

"It's a mongoose," Mom told us. "It might carry

rabies."

My heart pounded harder. Rabies. That's deadly.

"If it comes at us, run back to camp. Only rabid mongooses attack people," Mom said.

The mongoose ate all of Mom's dried apricots. It nosed around my backpack. As it went from pack to pack and back again, it would stop and stare at us with its beady eyes. We could see its sharp teeth.

"It probably smelled all of the candy bars that you had in your backpack," I hissed at Tomas.

After it finished our snacks, it decided we looked interesting. As it walked toward us, Mom shouted, "Run!"

Tomas and I bolted toward camp. Mom threw a large rock at the mongoose. I think she hoped to scare it so we would have time to get away.

The rock made the mongoose angry and it lunged at Mom.

"Mom!" I yelled. "Tomas get some sticks and rocks! Throw them!"

Tomas and I grabbed everything we could find and chucked it at the mongoose. He spit and hissed at us. Tomi threw a larger rock that landed on the mongoose's tail. It shrieked and dashed into the underbrush.

"Let's get out of here!" Mom said. We ran all the way back to camp.

"Did it bite you, Mom?" I asked after we caught our breath.

"No, it missed. But it sure tried hard," she said.

"Jake!" Mom called out.

"Yes, Dr. Perez?" Jake said as he walked across camp.

"Jake, take the Jeep and drive to the ranger station right away. File a report so they know we met a mongoose. It might have rabies."

"Yes, ma'am," Jake said and hopped in the Jeep.

"We'll let the rangers handle that mongoose," Mom said. "They'll track it down and trap it."

Bio Bay

Mom's research trip was successful. The team collected data about the Antillean crested hummingbird. After the mongoose scare, Mom's cameras captured the hatch of two healthy hummingbird chicks. Mom was excited about sharing her research with other scientists when she returned to Chicago.

After packing up camp and saying our goodbyes to Dr. O'Malley, Ben, and Jake, Dad suggested we spend our last night in Puerto Rico doing something special. We rented kayaks to explore Bio Bay. Tomas and I didn't know what a bio bay was. I trusted Dad when he told us it would be cool.

"It sounds like a biohazard," Tomas said sarcastically. "Like a toxic waste dump."

"Give it a chance. You've had fun so far," Dad said.

Tomas was tired and seemed a little grouchy.

"We'll see the bioluminescent bay best after dark," Dad said. We waited until the sun completely set before we paddled out through a mangrove tunnel.

"This is spooky," whispered Tomas.

"Just paddle close to us," Mom advised.

We heard the gentle sound of water lapping as our paddles cut through the bay.

"We're almost there," Dad said, turning his kayak.

After a few more minutes of paddling, we came out of the mangrove tunnel. We only had moonlight as our guide. "Here we are, in the Bio Bay," Dad said proudly. The water rocked us in our kayaks.

"My arms are sore from paddling," Tomas grumbled. "We're here. Are we done yet? Can we go now?"

"What's wrong with you?" I asked Tomas.

"Nothing. I just want to go back to the hotel."

I knew something was wrong with Tomas. This wasn't normal for him. Maybe he didn't feel well.

"Splash your paddle in the water," Dad said.

I hit the water with my paddles. The water lit up like it was charged with electricity. Neon blue flashes of light rippled across the water!

"Do it again," Dad said.

I did and the water lit up again. We were soon surrounded by glowing water. Tomas perked up.

"Awesome," he whispered.

"How does the water do this?" I asked Mom.

"It's the microscopic plankton that live in the water. They are bioluminescent. They glow," she said.

"It's magic," Tomas said. Even though Tomas sounded like a little kid, I agreed with him. It did look like magic.

"This has been an amazing trip," I said to Mom.

"Yes, honey, it has been amazing," Mom sighed and leaned back in her kayak, stretching and smiling.

They let us splash the water with our paddles for a while. We turned to paddle out of the bay when another group of kayakers appeared.

"Let's head back and enjoy a quiet evening," Dad said.

We followed him back through the mangrove tunnel, listening to the insects and frogs singing in the night.

At the hotel, guests gathered around the pool for an evening swim and live music. Tomas looked curiously around the crowd.

"What are you doing?" I asked him. "You look like you've never seen people before."

He shook his head at me but didn't say anything. Then he raced to catch up with Mom and Dad.

He stopped them and pointed to the pool. I saw Mom shrug her shoulders and nod.

Tomas ran to the pool. What was he up to? I trailed behind him. He turned to look at Mom and Dad, like he was making sure they weren't watching him. He edged around the pool. I followed, careful to stay in the shadows, out of his sight.

Tomas yanked six hibiscus flowers off a bush. What was he doing? Destroying the hotel property? He glanced around nervously again and checked his wristwatch.

"Tomas," a girl's high pitched voice rang across the courtyard. It was Carmen. Tomas waved to her and she ran to him. Ah ha! I thought. That's why he didn't want to waste time at Bio Bay. He had a date.

Because of course I must look after my twin brother, I hid in the bushes and watched them. Tomas gave Carmen the hibiscus flowers he'd taken from the hotel pool deck. Carmen tucked one of the flowers behind her ear. They talked quietly on a bench. Carmen laughed a lot. Tomas looked like a lovesick puppy.

I couldn't really hear what they were saying so I crept closer.

"I will miss you when you go back to Chicago," Carmen said quietly.

"Me too," Tomas answered.

"I meant it when I said you better call or write."

"I will," Tomas promised.

They sat silently for a moment.

"Here," Carmen said. "A good-bye gift for you." She reached into her bag and handed Tomas a long, rolled object.

Tomas unrolled the present. It was a large t-shirt that said "I Left My Heart in Puerto Rico" on the front.

"When you wear it, think of me," Carmen giggled.

Tomas blushed again. He nodded, staring at the ground.

"I will. Thanks," he mumbled, twisting the shirt in his hands awkwardly.

I burst out laughing. I couldn't help it. I sounded like a donkey. I slapped my hand over my mouth.

"What was that?" Tomas asked, startled.

"I don't know, but it came from over there," Carmen pointed toward where I was hiding in the bushes.

Oh no, I thought. They would see me and Tomas would freak out. I tried to back away through the bushes, but my shirt got caught. Tomas got off the bench and moved toward where I was. I cowered low, trying to make myself invisible.

Tomas rustled the bushes. He peered down at me.

"Tomas, what is it?" Carmen called.

"Nothing. Just a big stupid bird," he replied.

"Get lost. Now!" he hissed at me, his eyes narrowed. He looked furious.

I shook my head no.

"Go or I'll tell Mom and Dad you were sneaking around," he said through clenched teeth.

"Like you?" I asked.

"Tomas, who are you talking to?" Carmen asked.

"Uh, no one. I'm just sending a text message," Tomas pretended to type on his phone. "It's my mom," he lied.

"Go away, you're ruining it. Please?" he said, putting his hands together as if he were begging. Then he turned and rejoined Carmen on the bench.

I was getting hot and itchy in the bushes anyway so I crept back out to the pool deck to wait for Tomas after his date.

Later, Tomas walked back to the pool with Carmen. He held her hand and she gave him a peck on the cheek as she left. Turning, he saw me sitting on a lounge chair.

"Why do you try to ruin everything?" he asked.

"I don't," I snapped.

"Yes, you do. I can't have any privacy."

"You're the one who's sneaking around, acting all suspicious," I replied.

"Was not."

"Uh, yeah you were. I had to make sure you weren't in trouble."

"You're nosy," Tomas said.

"You'd do the same to me, if I was on a date."

"It wasn't a date."

"Looked like one to me."

Tomas clenched his fists. "It wasn't a date."

"With your girlfriend," I teased.

"We're just friends. I was just saying good-bye," Tomas looked sad. I decided to let it go.

Home

. . . .

"Wake up, sweetie," Mom nudged my shoulder. I rubbed my eyes, squinting at the morning sunlight.

"What time is it?" I mumbled, yawning.

"Time to get up and catch an airplane," Mom said cheerfully.

"Ugh," I moaned. Puerto Rico was incredible, even the soggy rainforest camp. I wasn't ready to leave the island and go back to Chicago. I knew Tomas wasn't ready to leave, either. He loved the hot tropical weather, the water, and the hearty meals of beans and rice. He loved Carmen. I giggled at the thought.

"We leave in an hour. If you want to shower and eat breakfast, you better hurry," Mom said as she rubbed my back. I rolled to the side of the bed. "Fine. I'm up," I said as I sat up and plunked my feet on the tile floor.

Tomas woke up earlier than I did. He was helping Dad pack the rest of our bags.

"Time to load the car," Dad said as he saw me stumbling to the bathroom. "Don't dilly-dally," Dad sang out as I walked by him.

Despite my feet dragging, we made it to the airport on time. The flight was long so I napped. Tomas stayed awake, organizing the photos from our Puerto Rico adventure on his laptop. He had a few photos of Carmen.

Mom woke me up as the airplane touched down in Chicago.

"We're home," she said brightly. I looked out the window. Although it was April, the sky was slate gray. The trees were bare. After spending three months in the glow of Puerto Rico, Chicago, from the sky, looked bleak and dreary.

"Home sweet home," Dad said as he unlocked our apartment door. He was right. It had been so long since we'd left for Puerto Rico, it was comforting to be back in a familiar place with all of our things. I curled up on the sofa, snuggling with the throw pillows. Tomas plopped down beside me. As he slid his phone in his pocket, I saw an image of Carmen on the screen.

"Still lovesick?" I asked him.

"Be quiet. Hand me that remote control," he demanded. "It's time to watch good old American cable TV."

"You better call her or email her, you know," I whispered to Tomas.

"Shush," he said, rolling his eyes. Mom came into the living room.

"I'm glad you kids have already adjusted back to life on the mainland," she laughed, sitting down on the sofa with us.

"I have a delicious idea," Dad said from the kitchen.

Twenty minutes later, with gooey, hot pizza cheese dripping from my mouth, I struck a Flamenco dancer pose and grinned. It was good to be home, but I knew it wouldn't be for long. That thought made me happy.

"So when is our next adventure?" I asked.

Marisol's Travel Journal

January 6

Puerto Rico Rocks!

One of my favorite Puerto Rican foods—and Tomas's too—is Arroz con Dulce, or Coconut Rice Pudding. Cinnamon, creamy, yummy! You can eat it hot or cold. Great for holidays!

Ingredients
$1^1/_2$ cups Medium Grain Rice
6 Whole Cloves
1 inch section of fresh ginger, peeled
1 fresh Cinnamon Stick
1 tsp. salt
1 can (15.5 oz.) Cream of Coconut
$^1/_2$ cup raisins
Whipped cream (optional)
Ground cinnamon (optional)
Berries (optional)

Directions
1. In medium bowl, add rice and cold water so the rice is covered by about two inches of water. Soak the rice for one hour. Rinse and drain.

2. Use a medium saucepan over medium-high heat, and bring to boil four cups of water, cloves, ginger, cinnamon and salt. Lower heat to medium low; simmer 10 minutes. Remove and discard spices. Reserve water in saucepan.

3. Stir cream of coconut into reserved water. Bring to a boil. Add reserved rice and raisins. Lower heat to medium low. Simmer, covered, until rice is soft and liquid is absorbed, about 15 to 20 minutes. Move rice pudding

to large dish; place in the refrigerator to get cool.

4. When ready to eat, scoop pudding onto plate. You can add ground cinnamon, berries, and whipped cream on top.

Fun Facts About Puerto Rico

Capital City: San Juan

Languages: Spanish and English

Population: More than three million people, plus about five million tourists each year

Climate: Puerto Rico is tropical. The temperature is usually about 80 degrees Fahrenheit (27 degrees Celsius).

Famous People:
Rosario Ferré (writer/poet)
Tito Puente (Jazz musician)
Pedro Rodriquez (scientist)
Chi Chi Rodriquez (golfer)
Jorge Posada (baseball player)

Events and Holidays

Christmas, Epiphany (January 6)
Ash Wednesday
Easter
Festival of San Juan Bautista-Patron Saint (June)
Constitution Day (July 25)
Discovery of Puerto Rico by Christopher Columbus (November 19)

Landmarks

El Morro
Where I tricked Tomas!

The other fort, Castillo San Cristobal is close by.

Awesome swimming at La Mina Falls. Water is usually a cool 65 degrees Fahrenheit (18 degrees Celsius)!

Arecibo Observatory
Where Tomas and I got into big trouble—major spot for science and research.

Now and Then

San Juan was founded in 1521 by the Spanish and was an important military post in the Caribbean. Today, it is a busy, modern city. More than 400,000 people live in San Juan. Tourism is one of its biggest industries.

Discussion Questions

1. Describe the history of Puerto Rico. Who settled the island? Who controls the island now?

2. Name the natural wonders that Marisol and Tomas experienced.

3. Marisol and Tomas learned about salsa dancing and flamenco dancing. Describe, in your own words, what the dances and music were like. Would you like to learn how to dance?

4. Name some of the discoveries that were made at the Arecibo Observatory. Now, do more research. Describe these discoveries in more detail. What did those discoveries teach you?

5. Think about the precautions that the family had to take while they were camping in El Yunque. Describe what they needed to do to survive in the wilderness. Why did they have to follow these rules?

6. At the Bio Bay, what caused the water to glow?

7. Why is Puerto Rico known as the Isle of Enchantment?

Vocabulary

Learn Spanish like Marisol and Tomas!
Practice using these Spanish words in everyday
conversations. Teach your friends these words, too!

arroz (ar-ROZ): rice
con (CON): with
gracias (grah-SEE-uhs): thanks
hola (Oh-la): hello, hi
Madre (ma-DREE): mother
niños (NEEN-yohs): children
no (noh): no
Padre (pa-DREE): father
pollo (pol- YOH): chicken
señor (SEEN-your): mister
señora (SEEN-your-AH): miss or missus
sí (SEE): yes

Websites to Visit

www.timeforkids.com/destination/puerto-rico
www.naic.edu/general/
www.fs.usda.gov/elyunque

About the Author:

Precious McKenzie lives in Montana and teaches writing to college students. She loves to help her college students become stronger writers. When she is not helping her students, Precious enjoys using her imagination to tell funny stories in books for children.

About the Illustrator:

Becka Moore studied Illustration for Children's Publishing in the North of Wales at Glyndwr University. She has since moved back home to Manchester where she works under the strict supervision of two very mischievous cats, doodling away and drinking far too much coffee.